Now You See Him, Now You Don't

Look for more

titles:

Now You See Him, Now You Don't

by Megan Stine

from the series created by
Robert Griffard
& Howard Adler

HarperEntertainment
An Imprint of HarperCollinsPublishers

A PARACHUTE PRESS BOOK

A PARACHUTE PRESS BOOK

Parachute Publishing, L.L.C.
156 Fifth Avenue
Suite 302
New York, NY 10010

Published by
HarperEntertainment
An Imprint of HarperCollins*Publishers*
10 East 53rd Street, New York, NY 10022-5299

TWO OF A KIND books created and produced by Parachute Press, L.C.C., in cooperation with Dualstar Publications, a division of Dualstar Entertainment Group, Inc., published by HarperEntertainment, an imprint of HarperCollins Publishers.
Cover photograph courtesy of Dualstar Entertainment Group, Inc. © 2002

ISBN 0-06-106661-3

First printing: February 2002

Printed in the United States of America

Visit HarperEntertainment on the World Wide Web at
www.harpercollins.com

10 9 8 7 6 5 4 3 2 1

CHAPTER ONE

"I'm in heaven," Mary-Kate Burke announced as she rushed through the doors of the White Oak cafeteria. "I've just had the most awesome afternoon of my entire life!"

Mary-Kate's twin sister Ashley glanced up from the powdered doughnut she was eating. She and a group of their friends were just finishing lunch. "Where have you been?" Ashley asked.

"And what's his name?" Samantha Kramer joked. "There must be a guy involved if your day was that good."

What's his name? Mary-Kate's eyes twinkled. "Well," she said, "actually his name is Sugar."

1

Ashley sputtered powder in Mary-Kate's direction. "You spent the afternoon with a guy named Sugar?"

"Say it, don't spray it," Mary-Kate complained. "And Sugar is not a guy. He's a horse."

"A horse?" Ashley asked.

"The best horse ever," Mary-Kate declared. "I rode him all afternoon, and he was perfect!"

"I didn't know we had horseback riding at White Oak," Samantha said. White Oak Academy was the all-girls boarding school they attended in New Hampshire.

"We don't," Mary-Kate explained as she took off her parka and squeezed next to Ashley on the bench.

"And I didn't know you rode," Phoebe Cahill said. Phoebe was Ashley's roommate. The girls were twelve years old and in the seventh grade.

"I started taking riding lessons back in Chicago when I was six," Mary-Kate said.

"She used to compete in show jumping," Ashley added. "Her room back home is filled with riding ribbons and trophies."

"I wish we did have riding here." Mary-Kate sighed. "I've missed it so much. My friend

2

Charlotte heard me talking about it in gym the other day. So she introduced me to her friend Sean. His family owns the Starbright Stables—right down the road. He said I could come over anytime I want to help him exercise the horses."

"It's funny that we're talking about horses," Phoebe said. "I just bought the greatest riding outfit. Vintage 1940s."

Mary-Kate rolled her eyes. Phoebe Cahill loved anything vintage. With her antique blue glasses, Phoebe herself looked as if she were living in the past. In fact, the only thing new in her room was her toothbrush!

"Sean wasn't there today," Mary-Kate went on. "So J.D.—he's one of the other stable boys—let me ride Sugar. Honestly, Ashley, he is the sweetest and smartest horse. Even you could ride him with no trouble!"

Ashley laughed. "I don't think so."

"What's the matter, Ashley?" Samantha asked. "Don't you like horses?"

"Sure, I like horses," Ashley said. "They just don't seem to like me."

"That's because you never learned to ride the right way," Mary-Kate said. "But you'd love Sugar,

Ashley. He's the smartest horse I've ever ridden. And I've ridden a lot of horses." She smiled, remembering how well Sugar had responded to every command. "He's perfect." She sighed.

"Who's perfect?" a boy's voice behind Mary-Kate asked.

Mary-Kate whirled around. Ross Lambert and three of his friends were standing near the bulletin board behind her.

Ross was Ashley's boyfriend and a student at Harrington Academy, the all-boys school down the road.

Ashley jumped to her feet and gave Ross a big smile. "She's talking about a horse," she explained.

"What are you guys doing here?" Mary-Kate asked the boys.

"We came to put up these posters," Ross said. He reached into the bag he had slung over his shoulder. "The annual magic show is coming up." He pulled out a glossy poster showing a magician's top hat and magic wand.

"I heard something about that," Mary-Kate said. "It's for charity, right?"

Ross nodded. "It's a pretty big deal. People come from all the towns around here to see the show."

Elliot Weber, one of the guys with Ross, added, "Each magic act is performed by a team—a Harrington guy and a White Oak girl. It's been a tradition."

Ross turned around to tack the poster to the bulletin board. "We've got to hurry up and choose partners," he said. "The show is only a few weeks away." He smoothed the poster and turned back to face Ashley. "I already know who I want for a partner." He leaned close to Ashley and waggled his brown eyebrows, grinning. "Got any good tricks up your sleeve?"

"Me?" Ashley's face lit up. "Not yet, but I can find one if I have to."

"That's okay," Ross said. "I know a great trick we can do together. So we're a team?"

Ashley shook his hand. "We're a team."

"I want to be in the magic show, too," Mary-Kate said. "I already know one magic trick!" She grabbed the rest of Ashley's doughnut. "Now you see it—" She popped the doughnut in her mouth. "Now you don't!"

Everyone laughed. Mary-Kate looked at the three boys who had come with Ross. *Would one of them be a good magic partner?* she wondered.

There was Elliot Weber, a tall, pale boy with short brown hair who was in her biology class. He was smart and very competitive.

He might be a good partner, Mary-Kate thought. Knowing Elliot, he'd want to make sure his trick was the best in the show.

Then there was Max Dorfman. He was short, with dark curly hair. He was shy and Mary-Kate didn't know him very well. The third boy was Marty Silver, who was always tripping over his own feet.

"I need a partner," Max said softly. "I'm going to pull a rabbit out of a hat."

Phoebe leaped to her feet. "I'll work with you! I love rabbits."

"Great," Max said. He gave a shy shrug and looked away.

"What kind of an act should we do?" Ashley asked Ross.

Ross shot her a smile. "I'm going to cut you in half," he said.

Ashley's jaw dropped. "You're kidding, right?"

"No, I'm serious," Ross said. "My uncle used to do magic tricks and he told me how the trick works."

Ross lowered his voice. Ashley and Mary-Kate

6

leaned in so that they could hear. "He's got this special box," he whispered. "You have to cram yourself into a weird position so I can saw you in half without, you know, a lot of screaming and stuff."

"Very funny," Ashley said. "But seriously. Is it safe?"

"Totally," Ross said. "We're going to be the stars of the show!" he announced loudly.

"In your dreams!" Elliot shouted.

"What does that mean?" Ross asked.

"It means my trick is going to be way better than yours," Elliot bragged. "Just wait and see."

"What is your trick?" Ross demanded.

"Like I said, wait and see," Elliot said.

Mary-Kate tapped Elliot on the shoulder. "Can I be your partner?"

He pulled her aside. "That depends," he whispered. "Got any good ideas?"

"You mean you don't have a trick?" Mary-Kate's eyebrows shot up.

"Shhh! Not so loud!" Elliot said. "I know a lot of good tricks, but I need a really great one."

Mary-Kate racked her brain, trying to remember magic tricks she'd seen. "How about pulling a coin from behind my ear?"

Elliot rolled his eyes. "Try again," he said.

"Putting me in a box and making me disappear?" she suggested.

"Bor-ing," Elliot said. "I need to do something special. Something really different."

Mary-Kate thought for a minute. *What can we do that no one else can?* she wondered.

"I've got it!" Mary-Kate cried. "Elliot, what if I said I could teach a horse to do magic tricks?" She told Elliot all about Sugar.

Elliot smiled and stuck out his hand for Mary-Kate to shake. "I'd say welcome to the team!"

CHAPTER TWO

"Aren't you coming?" Ashley stood in the doorway to Mary-Kate's dorm room in Porter House the next afternoon. "The magic show rehearsal started ten minutes ago. We're late!"

Mary-Kate glanced up from the book she was reading. "Go ahead without me," she told Ashley. "Elliot and I aren't ready to rehearse yet. We've got a few details to work out first."

"Whatever you say," Ashley said. She glanced around her sister's room, staring at the softball trophies and posters of Derek Jeter and Sammy Sosa. Mary-Kate and her roommate, Campbell Smith, had totally different tastes than she and

9

Phoebe did. Ashley's room was decorated with posters of poets and piles of soft throw pillows.

"Tell me all about it when you get back," Mary-Kate said.

"You got it," Ashley promised. "I'll see you later."

Ashley hurried down the steps of Porter House and dashed outside. A cold gust of wind whipped her long blond hair into her face. She ran across the snow-covered lawn to the shuttle bus stop just as the bus pulled up.

A few minutes later, it dropped her off at an old ivy-covered building that was Harrington's gymnasium and auditorium.

A sign on the door said: MAGIC SHOW REHEARSAL TODAY—NO ADMITTANCE.

Ashley tried the door. It was locked. *How am I supposed to rehearse if I can't get in?* she wondered.

She knocked as hard as she could. Finally the door opened a crack, and a boy's head peeked out.

"Jeremy?" Ashley said. Her cousin Jeremy was a student at Harrington. "Why is the door locked? Let me in!"

"No can do," Jeremy said. "The magicians are rehearsing. It's all top secret. No one's allowed in."

Ashley rolled her eyes. Her cousin Jeremy was the family jokester. He could also be the family pain. "I'm supposed to be in there right now," Ashley insisted. "Ross and I are doing an act together."

"Oh." Jeremy opened the door a little more. "Why didn't you say so?" He was wearing a black top hat and a cape.

"I'm the master of ceremonies for the show," Jeremy bragged. "I'm going to do a few jokes between acts."

"That's great," Ashley said. "Here's one for you. What wears a top hat and a cape and looks like a geek?"

Jeremy smirked. "Very funny," he said as he let her in.

Ashley followed Jeremy into the large old auditorium. The lights were dim in the back of the room, and Ashley had to squint at first to see what was happening.

"Ross is up there on the stage," Jeremy said. "Everybody's got a little space to practice in."

Ashley glanced around and saw groups of kids scattered all over the stage and in the orchestra seats.

Phoebe was standing halfway up the aisle. She

11

was petting Max Dorfman's white rabbit.

Ashley waved to Phoebe and hurried over to Ross.

"Hi," he said. "Where have you been?" He flashed her a smile.

Ashley's heart gave a little jump. "Sorry I'm late," she answered quickly. "I was waiting for Mary-Kate, but it turned out she isn't coming." She eyed the long black box that Ross had set up on a big table. "This is the magic box?" she asked. "What do I do?"

Ross bowed and gestured as if he were holding a car door open for her. "Hop in," he said.

Ashley gulped. The box looked complicated. From a distance, you couldn't tell that there was a secret compartment inside. But up close Ashley could see it.

And then Ashley spotted a gigantic saw lying on the floor. "You aren't going to use that—are you?" she squeaked.

"What's the matter?" Ross teased. "Don't think I can...cut it?"

He bent over and picked up the saw. "Doesn't it look real?" he asked. "It's actually totally harmless. The blade is made of rubber."

"Phew!" Ashley touched the rubber blade, just to

make sure. "But seriously, how am I supposed to get in that box?"

"Like this." Ross flipped some latches and all the sides of the box folded down flat. Now it was easy for her to slide in and lie down.

Ashley hopped up on the table and stretched out flat on her back. Then Ross closed the sides of the box around her and put the lid on top.

One end had two holes where her feet stuck out. The other end had a hole for her head.

The lid of the box and the sides were hinged together. In the middle of the box, near Ashley's waist, was a narrow slit just wide enough for the blade of a saw to fit through. At the slit, the box could be separated into two sections.

"Great," Ross said after he had locked her inside. "I'm going out for a pizza now. See you later!" He turned and started to walk away.

"Ross, don't you dare leave me in here!" Ashley called after him. She knew he was just kidding, but even the thought of being trapped in the box still made her really nervous.

"I'm just joking," Ross said, coming back and picking up the saw.

Ashley braced herself as he slid the saw down

13

through the slit in the middle of the box. The rubber blade touched her stomach.

"If that was a real saw, you would have taken two inches off my waist," Ashley said.

"Right," Ross agreed. "I wanted you to see how this works. The saw needs to go all the way through the box. So before I cut you in half, you've got to get your body out of the way."

"How?" Ashley asked.

"Put your right hand on the bottom of the box," Ross said. "There's a little lever there. When you pull it, the bottom will slide open and another compartment will open up underneath you."

Ashley felt around for the lever. Yup—there it was. She gave it a yank.

"Whoa!" she cried.

The minute she pulled the lever, a portion of the box underneath her fell away—and her rear end dropped down about twelve inches. Her whole body jerked toward the center of the box. Her chin hit one end of the wooden case, and her feet scraped against the top of the openings at the other end.

"Ow!" Ashley cried.

"Wait!" Ross said. "You weren't supposed to pull it yet."

"Great! Now you tell me!" Ashley groaned.

Ross opened all the latches and folded down the sides of the box again. Ashley hopped out.

"Look," he said. "I know this is tricky. My uncle said it will take some practice. But I'll be talking, so the audience won't notice you slipping down into the secret compartment. You also have to replace your real feet with fake feet."

"How will I do that?" Ashley asked.

Ross told Ashley how she'd get into the box and he'd close it up. Then he'd twirl the table around so the audience couldn't see her feet for a minute.

"Inside the box there will be two fake feet on long wooden poles," he told her. "All you do is pull your feet out of the holes at the end of the box. Then grab the long poles and stick the fake feet through the holes."

"Okay," Ashley said.

"I'll swing the table around again," Ross explained. "And you wiggle the fake feet—on the poles—with your hands."

Ross held out a pair of fake feet with clunky shoes and socks on them. Two long rods extended out of the ankles. He gripped the handles and moved the feet back and forth.

"No one will believe those are my feet," Ashley said.

"Why not?" Ross asked.

"Because everyone knows I wouldn't be caught dead in those shoes," Ashley said.

"You can dress up the feet with whatever shoes you want," Ross explained. "Just as long as they match the shoes you're wearing that night."

Ashley shrugged. "Doesn't sound that complicated," she said.

"Want to give it a shot?" Ross asked.

They ran through the trick once. Ross locked up Ashley inside the box. Then he turned the table so that her feet faced away from the audience. Ross made up some patter while Ashley pulled her feet out of the holes. She grabbed the wooden poles and tried to stick the fake feet through, but she couldn't do it in time. When Ross turned the table around, there were no fake feet sticking out of the hole—and no real feet, either.

"Ashley, what happened?" Ross asked.

"I need more time to switch the feet," Ashley complained. "You've got to talk longer."

"No, you've got to move faster," he insisted. "If I keep talking for too long, the audience will suspect something sneaky is going on."

Ashley sighed. She knew he was right, but it seemed impossible to go faster.

"Ashley, this is a great trick," Ross said. "No one will have a better trick than this. You've just got to practice, that's all."

They tried it again. And again. But they couldn't seem to get it right.

"What's the problem, Ashley?" Ross asked. He folded his arms. "It's not that hard."

Ashley frowned. "It *is* that hard," she argued. "We have to keep practicing."

They tried the trick a few more times. But each time it seemed like Ross was talking faster and faster.

"Ross, slow down!" Ashley said. "You're not giving me enough time. Nobody could do the trick that quickly."

"I bet anyone else could," Ross said.

Ashley bit her lip and glared at Ross. "Why are you being so stubborn?" she asked.

"Me!" he cried, throwing up his hands. "You're the one who's being stubborn. Just like you always are."

Ashley gasped. "What?" she cried.

"Forget it," Ross said. "I'm getting out of here."

He jumped off the stage and ran out of the auditorium. The heavy door slammed behind him.

Ashley stared after him. *I can't believe Ross and I have just had our first fight,* she thought. *Is our magic trick going to be okay?*

Are we going to be okay?

CHAPTER THREE

"I'll bet you five dollars," Elliot said. Mary-Kate turned to look at him as she slipped into her seat next to Jeremy in biology class.

Elliot sat across the aisle from her, one row back, at the end of a big lab table. Ross and some other guys were standing next to him.

"I'll bet five dollars my magic act gets more applause than Ross's," Elliot bragged with a grin.

Mary-Kate sighed. *Why does Elliot have to turn everything into a competition?* she wondered.

"You're on," Ross said, sticking out his hand to shake on the deal.

"Check this out." Elliot reached into his backpack and pulled out a rolled-up poster. He unrolled it to show to Ross and the other guys.

"I printed up a bunch of these yesterday while you were busy trying to saw your girlfriend in half," Elliot told them.

Mary-Kate gasped. The poster showed a picture of a horse with the words DON'T MISS THE HIGHLIGHT OF THE MAGIC SHOW, SUGAR THE WONDER HORSE!

"I plastered them all over town yesterday," Elliot said. "Mary-Kate and I are going to blow everyone out of the water!"

Mary-Kate hurried over to Elliot. "Elliot, why did you do that?" she demanded in a low voice. "We should make sure the trick will work before we start advertising it!"

"What's the problem, Mary-Kate?" Elliot asked. "You told me you could make Sugar do magic tricks. You said you had a plan."

"I do," Mary-Kate replied. "Sugar's a great horse, and I know I can train him. But he's not mine. I need to ask permission to borrow him for the show."

"So ask," Elliot said. "I'm sure the owner will say yes. The show's for charity—everybody in town supports it."

"I was planning to go to the stable this afternoon and ask," Mary-Kate said. "But I also have to figure out how to bring the horse into the auditorium—"

"I'll ask the headmaster for special permission," Elliot said. "Don't worry, Mary-Kate. It'll all work out."

Mr. Barber, the biology teacher, entered the room. "Let's take our seats, people," he bellowed.

Mary-Kate hurried back to her seat. Mr. Barber's head was bald on top and fringed with shaggy gray hair. He wore wire-rimmed glasses and a zip-up jacket. Jeremy leaned toward Mary-Kate as Mr. Barber unzipped his jacket.

"Let's see if he keeps the record going," Jeremy whispered.

Mr. Barber was famous at Harrington for wearing the same tie—a loud, goofy, extra-wide tie swirled with orange, red, blue, and purple—every single day. Every day for the last thirty years.

"Will we be seeing the tie again today?" Jeremy murmured like a sports announcer. "Can Mr. Barber keep up his record?"

Mr. Barber pulled his jacket off. There was the tie. "Yes!" Jeremy whispered. "The record grows!"

Mary-Kate giggled at her cousin.

21

While the class settled down, Mr. Barber said, "I have to go to the main office for a few minutes. I want all of you to pair off and study quietly for the quiz on the digestive system." He left the room.

"Mary-Kate!" Elliot called in a loud whisper. "Study with me."

Jeremy pursed his lips and made sloppy kissing noises. Mary-Kate jabbed her cousin with her elbow. "Stop being a pain," she whispered. Then she took a seat next to Elliot at the lab table.

"I'll quiz you first," Mary-Kate said.

"Forget the quiz," Elliot said. "We need to talk about our trick for the magic show. Let's hear your plan."

Mary-Kate nodded excitedly. She'd gone to the library and read a few magic books. She'd found a great trick that they could use with a horse.

"It's a card trick," she explained. "You tell me to pick a card, and I'll pick one out of the deck. You won't be able to see it because you'll be blindfolded. After I pick the card, I'll show it to the audience—and to Sugar. Then I'll put it back in the deck and take the blindfold off you."

Elliot nodded. "A card trick—I love it. Go on."

"You shuffle the deck and do some hocus-pocus," Mary-Kate said. "Pretty soon you say 'I think I've found your card,' and you show it to me."

"I think I know this trick," Elliot said. "But where does the horse come in?"

"I'll say 'Why don't you ask the horse if it's the right card?' Then Sugar will nod his head yes when you show him the card!"

"Brilliant!" Elliot said. "But how can you train a horse to recognize fifty-two different cards?"

Mary-Kate smiled and lowered her voice to a really soft whisper. "I can't. That's part of the trick."

"What do you mean?" Elliot asked.

"I'll train him to nod his head yes if you hold up the card with your left hand," Mary-Kate explained. "I know Sugar can do it. I once trained a horse to do something like this, and he wasn't as smart as Sugar is."

"Mary-Kate, this trick is going to be even better than I thought!" Elliot said. "I know another trick we can add to this one—it will really get the crowd going. I'll show Sugar the wrong card two or three times at first—on purpose. Then, finally, I'll pull the right card out of a sealed envelope. The horse will nod yes. Then I'll hold the card up to the audience. They'll go wild!"

"But, Elliot, how do you get the right card

into the sealed envelope?" Mary-Kate asked.

Elliot pretended to lock his lips. "I'll never tell," he said, his eyes dancing. "Magicians' secret."

"Excellent," Mary-Kate said. "I'll just teach Sugar to shake his head no if you hold up the card with your right hand. Now we just have to figure out how to get Sugar onstage."

"I'll try and get permission from the Harrington headmaster today," Elliot told her.

Mary-Kate nodded. "And I'll ask my friend at the stables if I can borrow Sugar."

"Right," Elliot agreed. "When you get to the auditorium, there's a back door behind the stage. We can lead the horse in through the door and up a ramp to the stage."

"I think it might work!" Mary-Kate cheered. "This is going to be awesome. We'll have one of the best tricks in the show!"

As soon as class was over, Mary-Kate rushed over to Ashley. "I've got to tell you about the trick I'm doing with Elliot," she said.

Ashley gathered up her books and they started to walk out the door. "I hope he's not sawing you in half," she grumbled. "Believe me, it's not as easy as it looks."

"No—we're doing a card trick," Mary-Kate

whispered. "And I'm going to train Sugar to recognize the card!"

"You're kidding!" Ashley said. "You guys are using a horse in your trick?"

"Yup," Mary-Kate said. "But first I've got to talk Sean into letting me borrow Sugar for the show. Can you come with me to the stables this afternoon? We can go riding for a little while, too."

Ashley shook her head. "No way. You know me and horses."

"But it would be soooo much fun to go riding together," Mary-Kate said. "It'll be like our own special sister time."

Ashley hesitated. "Well . . ." she began.

"Pretty please?" Mary-Kate said sweetly.

"I guess it could be fun," Ashley said. "But you'd better make sure I don't have any problems with that horse!"

"Don't worry," Mary-Kate said. "I'll make sure everything goes perfectly."

Sean waved as he walked toward Mary-Kate at the stables later that day.

"Hi, Sean." Mary-Kate waved back. "This is my sister, Ashley."

"Hi," Ashley said. She jumped as a horse flicked her with his tail.

"I have a couple of favors to ask," Mary-Kate went on.

Sean raised his eyebrows. "What's up?"

"I was wondering if I could borrow one of your horses for a magic trick I'm doing in the Harrington magic show," Mary-Kate asked.

Sean listened while she told him all about the show and the card trick she and Elliot wanted to do.

"That sounds really cool," Sean said. "I'll check with my dad, but I think it'll be okay."

"Great, thanks!" Mary-Kate said.

"What's the second favor?" Sean asked.

"I was wondering if Ashley could ride with me today," Mary-Kate said.

"Sure." Sean headed into the stables. He walked down the row of horses. "Let's see. Which horse would be good for her?"

"Got any of the kind that rocks back and forth?" Ashley asked.

Mary-Kate giggled. "You're going to love Sugar," she told her sister. She turned to Sean. "Can Ashley ride him today?"

Sean stared at Mary-Kate. "Sugar?" he said. "Are

you sure you want me to get Sugar for you?"

"Yeah, why?" Mary-Kate asked, confused. "He's a great horse."

"You must be a really good rider," Sean said with a whistle. "I'll go saddle him up for you."

"Why is he saying that, Mary-Kate?" Ashley demanded as Sean walked away. Mary-Kate could tell she was getting nervous.

"I'm not sure," Mary-Kate said as they walked outside. "But would I let you get on an unsafe horse?"

"I hope not!" Ashley said as Sean headed toward them. He was leading a beautiful gray horse with a white patch on his right ankle. He also led a dappled brown horse toward Mary-Kate.

"This one's name is Chestnut," Sean said. "I thought you would have fun riding him, Mary-Kate."

He tied both horses to a fence, then started to walk away. "Will you guys be okay if I leave?" Sean called over his shoulder.

"Definitely," Mary-Kate said.

"Maybe," Ashley squeaked.

"Don't worry," Mary-Kate reassured her sister. "They wouldn't call him Sugar if he wasn't so sweet!"

Mary-Kate took Sugar's reins and held them for Ashley. "Climb on up!"

Ashley put her foot in the stirrup and heaved herself into the saddle. She clung to the horse's neck with both hands.

"Okay, take the reins," Mary-Kate said, handing them to her sister.

Ashley slowly reached forward. But just as she was about to grab the reins, Sugar started backing up and shaking his mane.

"Mary-Kate!" Ashley shrieked.

"Whoa!" Mary-Kate called, trying to steady the horse. She petted the horse's side.

Sugar whinnied. He pulled away and started to back up faster.

"I'm going to fall!" Ashley cried. She buried her face in the horse's neck as she held on. "Hellllp!"

Mary-Kate caught up with Sugar and grabbed the reins. She pulled hard enough to get Sugar's attention.

"Whoa, boy. Steady," she said firmly. The horse settled down a bit.

"Climb down, Ashley," Mary-Kate directed.

Ashley jumped off the horse. "Sweet? Well behaved?" she yelled at her sister. "Mary-Kate has the horse smell gone to your head?"

"I don't get it!" Mary-Kate said. "He was perfect the last time I rode him. Let me try."

She climbed onto Sugar's back. But as soon as she was seated, he started backing up again.

"Whoa!" Mary-Kate said. "Steady!"

Sugar calmed down. "Okay, now, boy," Mary-Kate said, stroking his neck. "Let's go for a walk around the corral."

She clicked her tongue and gave the signal for Sugar to start walking. But he wouldn't move. No matter what she did, he stood perfectly still.

"Well, at least it's not me," Ashley commented.

"I don't understand it," Mary-Kate said, climbing down. "I know this is the horse I rode the last time. He looks the same, but he's acting so different. . . ."

Mary-Kate tied Sugar to the fence and sat down on the grass. "Ashley, how am I going to teach Sugar to nod yes or no when I can't even get him to walk?" she asked.

"Magic?" Ashley suggested weakly.

From the corner of her eye Mary-Kate could see Sean strolling toward them.

"What's the trouble?" Sean asked, walking up to them.

"Sugar isn't behaving as well as I thought he would," Mary-Kate said. "I can't get him to move an inch. Are you sure this is Sugar?"

"It's Sugar all right," Sean said with a nod. "I'm not surprised he won't obey you. He's so stubborn that most people can't even get him out of his stable."

But how can that be? Mary-Kate thought. *He was so good the last time I rode him.*

"How am I going to train him for the magic show?" she wondered out loud.

"Do you have to do a horse trick?" Ashley asked. "Why don't you and Elliot do something else?"

"We can't." Mary-Kate groaned. "Elliot already plastered the town with posters about Sugar the Wonder Horse. Everyone will be expecting to see him!"

Ashley put her arm around Mary-Kate's shoulders. "I hate to say it, but if that's the horse you want to train, you're in big trouble."

CHAPTER FOUR

"Oh, Ashley," Phoebe gushed. "Don't you think he's the cutest thing you've ever seen?"

"Hmm?" Ashley asked. It was Saturday, and she and Phoebe were riding the shuttle bus into the small town near White Oak Academy. Ashley looked up from a book she had borrowed from Phoebe. It was a book of magic tricks, and Ashley was reading about how to cut a rope in half and then make it whole again.

Ashley leaned over Phoebe and glanced out the window of the shuttle bus. "Who's cute? Who are we looking at?"

"Not out there," Phoebe said. "I was talking

31

about the rabbit Max is using in our act."

Ashley turned to face her friend. "You've been talking about that rabbit all week," she said.

"I can't help it," Phoebe said. She leaned back on the brown leather seat. "I've never had a pet before. Besides, you've been talking about magic all week!"

"I know!" Ashley said. "I'm totally into it now." She'd been reading up on magic partly for fun—and partly because she was worried. She really wanted to get Ross's trick right at practice that afternoon. That way they wouldn't fight again.

The bus pulled onto Main Street. Ashley closed the book and put it in her tote bag.

"You know, Ashley," Phoebe said, buttoning her pea coat, "that poor bunny doesn't even have a name. Don't you think we should give him one?"

"Definitely," Ashley agreed. "Max bought him from the pet store a week ago. Why hasn't he named him yet?"

"I don't know," Phoebe said. "Maybe because he doesn't love the rabbit as much as I do." She paused, thinking of names. "What about Dickinson? After Emily Dickinson?"

"Dickinson?" Ashley rolled her eyes. They had an Emily Dickinson poster hanging in their room.

She was Phoebe's favorite poet. "Isn't that a little sophisticated for a rabbit?"

"Well, we can't call him Emily, because he's a boy. And I don't want to name him after Shakespeare," Phoebe said. Phoebe loved William Shakespeare's plays and sonnets. "I'm saving that for a dog—if my parents ever let me get one."

"Where is Max keeping the rabbit?" Ashley asked. "I thought Harrington didn't allow pets in the dorms."

"They don't. Max has been trying to hide him, but he says it's getting too hard," Phoebe said. She gave Ashley a big smile. "That's why I've offered to keep him in our room."

"What? Hel-lo!" Ashley cried. "Phoebe, White Oak doesn't allow pets in the dorms either."

"Don't think of him as a bunny," Phoebe reasoned. "We can pretend he's—a slipper!"

Ashley groaned under her breath. "Is there any way I'm going to change your mind?" she asked.

Phoebe shook her head. "Don't worry, Ashley. No one will ever know he's there. I'll keep him safe and sound."

"Okay," Ashley said. "But be careful, because if Ms. Viola finds out about this she's going to be really mad!" Ms. Viola was the housemother at Porter House.

The bus pulled into the stop and the girls climbed off. They were standing on the town's main street in front of a row of shops and cafés. A brisk, cold wind blew up the street. Ashley put on her white knit cap and started walking.

"Where should we go first?" Phoebe asked.

"How about the crafts store?" Ashley answered. "I want to get some sequins for my costume." She planned to wear a glamorous, sparkly outfit onstage, just like she'd seen in magic shows on TV.

"Look!" Phoebe cried. She pointed to a storefront a few buildings down. "They're having a sale at Winnie's! Can we go there first?"

Ashley knew this was Phoebe's favorite thrift store. Half her closet was filled with old corduroy pants, wild 1960s blouses, beaded 1930s dresses, and crazy fur hats. And the great thing was, she could put them all together and look amazing!

Phoebe stopped to gaze in the front window. "Maybe they've got some new vintage," she said excitedly.

"New vintage? Isn't that impossible?" Ashley teased.

Phoebe ignored her. "Wow—check out that fur-trimmed sweater!" she exclaimed, as they slipped into the warm store. "I've got to try it on."

Ashley wandered around the thrift shop while Phoebe tried on the sweater. Most of the clothes weren't Ashley's taste. But there were some cool old necklaces and earrings in a display case.

"Hey, Ashley, look!" Phoebe called out. "Isn't that Mr. Barber's tie over there?"

Ashley turned around. "Hey, it is!" she said. "Who would have thought they'd make two of those hideous things?"

Phoebe walked over and picked up the bright swirly tie. It was identical to the tie Mr. Barber wore to school every day.

"It must be from the sixties," Phoebe said, tilting her head and studying it. "It has that pop art look."

"It's making my eyes pop!" Ashley said.

"Want to buy it?" Phoebe asked. "We could get one of the guys to wear it to class as a joke."

"I only have enough money to buy my costume decorations," Ashley said.

She looked at the tie again. Then she thought of the magic trick she had read about on the bus—how to cut a rope in half and make it whole again.

"I'd love to use that tie in a magic trick," Ashley said. She didn't have to use a rope for that trick. A tie would work just as well.

"But I thought Ross was sawing you in half," Phoebe said.

"He is," Ashley agreed, hesitating a little. "But we're having trouble with it. Maybe we should have a backup if it doesn't work out. And even if it does, two tricks are better than one." She explained the rope trick to Phoebe.

"That's a funny idea—especially if you can get Mr. Barber to go along with it," Phoebe said. "Why don't you buy the tie? It's not expensive. I'll lend you the money."

"Thanks," Ashley replied.

Phoebe bought the fur-trimmed sweater and the tie, and the girls hurried down the street to the crafts store.

"I need a glamorous costume for the show," Ashley explained. "So I'm going to sew sequins to a black leotard I have."

When they reached the store, she went through the little boxes of sequins and shiny beads along the counter and picked some out.

Phoebe looked at her watch. "We've got to hurry.

Rehearsal for the show starts in half an hour."

Ashley paid for her sequins and the girls hurried to the shuttle bus. They got off at Harrington's campus instead of at White Oak.

The door to the auditorium was locked again, but after a few loud knocks, Jeremy opened the door.

"What's the secret password?" he asked them.

"Dorkface?" Ashley guessed.

"Dorkface *is* the password!" he said, letting them by. "How did you know?"

Ashley didn't answer. She said good-bye to Phoebe and rushed to the back of the stage. Ross was there waiting for her.

"Hey," she called, slipping out of her jacket and hat. She glanced at him, wondering if he was still mad at her.

"Hey," Ross replied. "We have to work really hard today. I'm starting to get freaked that we won't have our trick ready. We've got only a week until the show."

Ashley nodded. She could sense the tension between them. They'd never really made up since their fight.

For the next two hours Ashley tried her best to get into the secret compartment quickly. But each time Ross put the saw into the slot and pretended to cut her in half, she felt it hit her stomach.

"Come on, Ross," Ashley said. "You have to give me more time."

Ross looked at his watch. Ashley knew it was late. All the other students had already left the auditorium. She and Ross were the only ones left rehearsing.

"I'm talking for as long as I can." Ross frowned. "Maybe if you got in the box the way I told you to, we wouldn't have a problem."

"Maybe if you gave me better instructions, I would know what I'm doing," Ashley shot back. She paused, rubbing her forehead. *We've got to stop this arguing,* she thought. *I don't want to get into another fight.*

"Why don't I just practice by myself for a while?" Ashley suggested.

"Fine," Ross said. He walked off the stage and up the aisle. Then he left the auditorium and shut the door. Ashley stood on the stage, all alone in the auditorium.

"Fine," Ashley repeated. She began to calm down. Without Ross there, it was better. Ashley didn't feel so pressured. She could take her time to figure things out.

She started from the beginning. She climbed into

the box and pulled the lid shut. She put her feet through the holes in the end. Then she practiced pulling them out and switching the fake feet as fast as she could.

Yes! Ashley thought. This time she did it in about ten seconds. *Wait until I tell Ross.*

Ashley pushed on the top of the box to climb out. But the lid didn't budge.

"Come on," she grumbled. "Open!"

She gave another hard shove against the lid. It didn't move.

"Hey! Let me out of here," she called, banging on the box again from all sides. She tried to push open the sides, and then the top again.

It was no use. The box wouldn't open. She was trapped!

CHAPTER FIVE

"Help!" Ashley yelled as loud as she could. "Hellllp!"

She banged on the box a few more times in desperation. But it was no use. The box was locked. She was stuck.

What am I going to do now? she thought miserably.

"Ashley?" a voice called.

"Ross?" Ashley turned her head. "Ross! Get me out of here!"

Ross leaped onto the stage and unlocked the box. "I was on my way back to my dorm when I remembered that you couldn't unlock the box. So I ran all the way back here as fast as I could to get you out!"

Ashley jumped out of the box and shook her legs. It felt good to be able to move again. "I'm glad you remembered," she said. "I thought I was going to spend the night in that thing!"

Ross looked down at his sneakers. "I'm sorry, Ashley. And I'm sorry I got annoyed with you before."

"I'm sorry, too," Ashley said. "I know you just want the trick to be good."

"And I know you were trying your best," Ross admitted. "You were right—I need to give you a little more time."

They smiled at each other. The tension between them melted away. "Let's not fight anymore," Ashley said.

"Deal," Ross agreed. He grabbed her hand and held it for a second.

I can't believe we let such a silly thing come between us, Ashley thought. Then she remembered the rope trick.

"I came up with another trick, you know," Ashley said. "In case we couldn't get the box trick right."

"I'm sure we'll get it right eventually," Ross said.

"But what's your idea for the other trick?"

"Well, I read about this magic trick where you cut a rope in half and then put it back together," she explained. "The catch is that you need two pieces of rope that look identical."

"A rope trick?" Ross asked.

"Not exactly," Ashley said, grinning. "You know that tie Mr. Barber wears every day?"

Ross nodded. "The eye-popper? How could I miss it?"

"I bought one exactly like it at the thrift shop in town," she said. "What if I pretended to cut Mr. Barber's tie in half instead of a rope?"

Ross laughed. "Mr. Barber will flip out. His students will love it!"

Ashley laughed, too. "No kidding. It would be really funny."

"You know, Ashley," Ross said. "I'm sure the box trick is going to work—and it will be great. But that tie trick is hilarious. Why don't we do both tricks? Then our act will really rock!"

"All right," Ashley agreed. "I'll practice it in my room until I get it down perfectly."

Ross held Ashley's hand as they left the auditorium. She was so glad they'd made up. But in the back of her mind, there was still one thing that worried her.

She still hadn't mastered the box trick. And she hadn't even tried the tie trick yet.

The show is only a week away, she thought. *Will I be able to pull off both tricks in time?*

CHAPTER SIX

"So, did Ross like the tie trick?" Mary-Kate asked Ashley. The sisters were standing in the exercise ring at the Starbright Stables, waiting for Sean to bring Sugar out. Ashley was going to help Mary-Kate train Sugar.

"He loved it," Ashley said. "We're going to add it to our act. This afternoon I asked Mr. Barber if he wanted to be part of the act."

"Did he say yes?" Mary-Kate asked. She rubbed her mittened hands together in the chilly air.

"He was really excited," Ashley replied. "He said no one has asked him to be part of the magic show in twenty years."

44

"And he doesn't mind that you're going to use his tie?" Mary-Kate asked.

"Well," Ashley hesitated. "I didn't exactly mention that part. You know how he is about his tie. He's always patting it, and he kind of moves away if you get too close to it—like he's protecting it or something. But his tie won't be damaged in my trick. I'm sure it will be fine."

"Here he is," Sean said as he led a gray horse to the exercise ring. "You asked for Sugar, you got Sugar. Good luck."

"Thanks, Sean." Mary-Kate took Sugar's reins.

"I hope Sugar's in a better mood than he was last time," Ashley said.

"Me, too," Mary-Kate agreed. She explained to Ashley how the trick worked.

"We need to get Sugar to shake his head," she said. "Horses naturally shake their heads when a fly bites them. It's like a reflex. If a fly bites a horse on the neck, he shakes his head no. If the horse is bitten on the chest, he nods his head yes."

"What does that have to do with the trick?" Ashley asked.

"When you hold up a card in your right hand, I'll scratch Sugar's neck and he'll shake his head no.

45

When you hold up a card in your left hand, I'll scratch his chest and he'll nod his head yes."

"Cool," Ashley said. "So the scratch will act like the bug bite."

"Exactly," Mary-Kate replied. "After a while, just the sight of the card in someone's right hand or left hand should make him shake his head no or yes."

"Scratching him won't make him mad, will it?" Ashley asked, backing up.

"Nope," Mary-Kate replied. "So when I tell you to hold up a card, hold a card in front of him so he can see it. We'll do the right hand first, okay?"

Ashley glanced at the first card in the deck—a queen of hearts. "He doesn't charge when he sees red, does he?"

"Ashley, that's a bull, not a horse," Mary-Kate said. "Don't worry. Elliot will take over when he gets here."

Elliot had promised to come to the stables to rehearse the trick as soon as his wrestling practice was over. But Mary-Kate wanted to get a head start on training Sugar before he got there.

"Ready?" Mary-Kate held Sugar by the reins and stood on his left side. "Hold a card up in your right hand."

Ashley held up a card and said, "Is this your card?"

Mary-Kate scratched Sugar's neck. Sugar flicked his tail.

"That's weird," Mary-Kate said. "Every other horse I've known would shake his head. Let's try it again."

Ashley waved a card in her right hand. "Is this your card?" Mary-Kate scratched Sugar's neck again, a little harder this time.

Sugar snorted and reared up. "Stampede!" Ashley screamed.

Mary-Kate tightened her grip on Sugar's reins and calmed him down. "Don't panic," she told Ashley. "I must have scratched him a little too hard that time, that's all."

"Why don't you try teaching him yes?" Ashley suggested.

"Maybe that will be easier," Mary-Kate agreed. "Hold a card up in your left hand this time."

Ashley held up the card and repeated the question. Mary-Kate gingerly scratched Sugar on the chest. The horse bowed his head and butted Mary-Kate's hand with his nose.

Mary-Kate sighed with frustration. "I don't get

it. Why is Sugar having so much trouble with this?"
Mary-Kate had always trusted her instincts with
horses—and they'd usually been right. She'd never
misjudged one so badly before.

"Here I am!" Elliot walked into the exercise ring.
"Is this the wonder horse? How's it going?"

"Um, okay," Mary-Kate said. "We just started
training him."

"Let's see what you've got so far," Elliot said.
Ashley handed the deck of cards to him. He held
one up in his right hand. "Is this your card?" he
asked Sugar.

Mary-Kate scratched Sugar on the neck. Sugar
bucked slightly and spat at Elliot. The horse spit
landed in his hair.

"Hey!" Elliot cried. "What's he doing?"

Ashley burst out laughing. But Mary-Kate was
too worried to find it funny.

"We need a little more practice," she told him.

"Are you sure you know what you're doing?"
Elliot asked.

Ashley rushed to her sister's defense. "Hey—if
there's one thing Mary-Kate is an expert on, it's
horses. She'll work it out."

"It had better work out," Elliot said, "because

everybody in school is already buzzing about what a great act we have. But if this horse doesn't hurry up and learn this trick, we won't have an act!"

Mary-Kate didn't want to let everybody down. *Oh, Sugar,* she thought. *Was I wrong about you?*

"Give me some time alone with him," Mary-Kate said. "Maybe he'll be more obedient if he gets to know me better."

"All right, Mary-Kate," Elliot said. "But remember—the show is only two days away!"

Elliot and Ashley left. Mary-Kate struggled with Sugar. She tried everything she could think of. She spent the whole afternoon with him, but he made no progress. It was beginning to get dark when she finally decided to give up.

"It's hopeless." She sighed. She took the reins and led Sugar back into the barn.

Sean was cleaning out the next stall. He stopped sweeping when he saw her come in. "How did it go?" he asked.

"Terribly," Mary-Kate admitted. "I hate to say it, but I don't think I can train this horse. I'm going to have to tell Elliot I can't do the trick."

Sean looked sympathetic. "I still don't understand why you picked Sugar to train," he said.

"He never listens to anything anyone says."

"That's not true," Mary-Kate insisted. "The first time I rode him he did everything I wanted him to do. He was the perfect horse."

"Sounds like you're talking about my Sugar!" a girl's voice called out.

Mary-Kate turned around. She saw a girl dressed in gray stretch pants and a white sweater. Her long blond hair was held back with a black velvet headband.

"That's Darcy Boyd," Sean explained. "She goes to Maplewood Academy."

Maplewood Academy was another nearby school. Mary-Kate's softball team played against Maplewood sometimes.

"You have a horse named Sugar, too?" Mary-Kate asked.

Darcy nodded. "We keep him in our own stable behind our house."

"Have you ever kept your horse here?" Mary-Kate asked.

Darcy nodded. "A few weeks ago my parents and I went on vacation," she explained. "So we kept Sugar here." She stared at the horse Mary-Kate had brought in. "Actually, my Sugar is gray, too—in fact he looks an awful lot like that horse."

Sean smacked his forehead with his palm.

"Oh, man! Why didn't it click?" he said. "You rode the day J.D. was here, when I was gone. He probably put you on Darcy's horse so he'd get some exercise."

Mary-Kate stared at Sean. "I can't believe it," she cried. "This whole time I've been trying to train the wrong horse!"

CHAPTER SEVEN

"Sorry, Mary-Kate," Sean said. "I should have figured out that you were talking about a different horse. But when you asked for Sugar, I just assumed you meant our Sugar!"

"It's amazing how much this Sugar looks like my Sugar," Darcy commented. "Except for the marks on their ankles."

"What do you mean?" Mary-Kate asked.

"This Sugar has a white patch on his right ankle," Darcy pointed out. "My Sugar doesn't. Other than that, they're practically identical."

"Darcy, can I ask you a big favor?" Mary-Kate crossed her fingers behind her back. "Do you think

I could train your horse to be in the magic show at Harrington?"

Darcy's eyes lit up. "I went to that show last year," she said. "It was great!"

Mary-Kate told Darcy about Elliot's card trick. She explained that she wanted to train the horse to shake his head yes or no.

"What a neat trick!" Darcy said.

"So can Sugar be in the show with me?" Mary-Kate asked.

"I don't know," Darcy said, shaking her head. "Nobody ever trains Sugar but me."

"But think about it," Mary-Kate prodded. "Everyone will talk about how smart your horse is for months to come!"

Darcy grinned. "Okay. This could be fun. We can train him together."

"Great!" Mary-Kate sighed with relief.

"It shouldn't be hard to teach Sugar the trick. I teach him little tricks all the time," Darcy said.

"Terrific!" Mary-Kate said. "Thanks a million."

Darcy gave Mary-Kate her address. Mary-Kate would have to go to the Boyds' stable to work with the horse.

Mary-Kate said good-bye to Darcy and Sean.

Then she climbed onto the shuttle bus back to
school.

Thank goodness, Mary-Kate thought, dropping
into a seat. *Darcy saved our magic trick!*

*Now all I have to do is figure out a way to train a
horse—in two days!*

Ashley hurried to the Harrington auditorium.
She'd been practicing her tie-cutting trick all morning and was getting really good at it.

She found Ross onstage with Jeremy. They were
pushing Ross's box to the middle of the stage.

"There you are!" Ross said.

"Ross just told me he had to rescue you from this
box," Jeremy said. He grabbed his chest and flut-
tered his eyelashes. "My hero!"

Ashley frowned at her cousin. "You'd better
watch it," she said. "Or you're going to be locked in
there next."

"Ooh, I'm shaking," Jeremy said.

"Are you ready to practice, Ashley?" Ross
interrupted.

"Before we start, I want to show you the tie trick
I told you about," Ashley said. "I've got it down
pretty well. Wait till you see it." Ross nodded as she

took the loud colorful tie out of her pocket.

"Whoa!" Jeremy yelled when he saw the tie. "You stole Mr. Barber's tie."

"No, I didn't," Ashley said. "It just looks like Mr. Barber's tie."

She set the tie aside and pulled out two matching red ribbons. "Pretend this is Mr. Barber's tie," she said. Then she showed them the trick. First she took a top hat with two secret pockets—one on the left and one on the right—and placed it on the table. Then she cut one of the ribbons in half and stuffed it into the left pocket inside a top hat. She covered the hat with a scarf, said "Abracadabra," and showed the empty hat to the boys. Then she waved her hands over the hat and pulled out a red ribbon from the right pocket—whole and uncut.

Jeremy clapped. "Excellent!" Ross shouted. "That trick is going to bring down the house."

Ashley bowed. "Thank you, thank you."

"It's your trick, Ashley," Ross said. "You'll be the magician for it—and I'll be your assistant."

"Great!" Ashley said. Now they were more of a team than ever.

"But, Ashley, you're not going to cut Mr. Barber's tie in half, are you?" Jeremy asked.

Ashley explained that she was going to pretend to cut Mr. Barber's tie in half. But she would really be cutting the fake tie.

"You'd better not mess up that trick," Jeremy warned. "Barber freaks out if anyone even touches his tie."

"I know," Ashley said. "That's what makes the trick extra-funny."

"Once a student bumped into his tie with a chocolate ice cream bar," Jeremy went on. "Barber was so upset, he canceled class for the day so he could go to the dry cleaner."

"You made that story up," Ashley said. "Didn't you, Jeremy?"

"Okay, so I did," Jeremy admitted. "But I'd be extra careful if I were you."

"You're not going to get us in trouble," Ross asked. "Are you, Ashley?"

"Of course not," Ashley insisted. "This trick is a piece of cake. Nothing can possibly go wrong."

She flashed him a nervous grin. *At least, I hope nothing will go wrong,* she thought. *Or Mr. Barber will never forgive me—and neither will Ross!*

CHAPTER EIGHT

"Okay, Sugar." Darcy Boyd stood in front of her horse and held up a card in her right hand. "Is this your card?"

Mary-Kate was standing outside the Boyds' stable, holding Sugar—the good Sugar—by his reins. She gently scratched him on the neck. Sugar shook his head no.

"Good boy!" Mary-Kate cried. She fed him a carrot to reward him.

Darcy patted his nose. Mary-Kate rubbed the smooth gray hair on his neck. It really was amazing how much Darcy's horse looked like the other Sugar. But their personalities couldn't be more different.

Darcy and Mary-Kate practiced the trick with Sugar over and over again. Before long Sugar shook his head no without being scratched. All he needed was to see the card in Darcy's right hand and hear her ask the question.

"You're so lucky, Darcy," Mary-Kate said. "Sugar is a great horse."

"Isn't he?" Darcy agreed. "But you're really good with him, too, Mary-Kate. I can tell you know what you're doing—and so can Sugar."

Mary-Kate gave Sugar another piece of carrot.

"I think it's so cool we're teaching him this trick," Darcy added. "Sugar loves attention!"

"He'll get plenty of it at the magic show," Mary-Kate said. "Now let's teach him to say yes."

Sugar quickly learned to nod yes when Mary-Kate touched his chest. *This is really working!* Mary-Kate thought. She could feel her excitement growing.

This trick really is going to steal the show!

"Why did I ever agree to be your stand-in?" Ashley asked. She and Mary-Kate were on their way to the Harrington auditorium for the magic show dress rehearsal.

"Because you're my sister and you love me," Mary-Kate said. "And I promised you could borrow my brand-new sweater," she added.

Mary-Kate and Ashley walked into the auditorium and tossed their coats onto one of the seats. Mary-Kate scanned the room, looking for Elliot. About twenty people were there, waiting their turn to rehearse onstage.

"Hey, Mary-Kate." Elliot waved from the back row. "Over here."

Mary-Kate and Ashley walked up the aisle to join him.

"What's she doing here?" Elliot asked, eyeing Ashley suspiciously. "She's part of the competition."

"It's not a competition, Elliot," Mary-Kate said. "And I asked Ashley to stand in for Sugar."

"But how's the real horse doing?" Elliot asked. "Did you teach him the trick?"

"It's been going great," Mary-Kate told him. "Once Sugar nodded his head yes when I gave the signal for no, but every other time he was perfect."

"Okay," Elliot said. "But he'd better not mess up at the show. Everyone will be paying extra-close attention to us. I made sure that we're the grand finale!"

Elliot, Mary-Kate, and Ashley went up onto the stage. Jeremy was at a microphone, acting as the emcee. He was wearing his black cape and top hat.

"And now, ladies and gentlemen, let's give a huge hand to the one and only Elliot Weber!" Jeremy said.

Elliot walked out onto the stage wearing a wireless microphone clipped to his T-shirt.

"Thank you, thank you," he said, bowing. "Ladies and gentlemen, tonight I am going to perform an amazing feat of mind-reading using only a deck of cards. But first, allow me to introduce my partner, Mary-Kate Burke, and Sugar the Wonder Horse!"

That was Mary-Kate's cue. She hurried onto the stage, leading Ashley by a string tied around her wrist.

The kids watching from the audience all broke out laughing. Some of them whistled and hooted.

Ashley turned bright red. "You owe me big-time for this one!" she whispered to Mary-Kate.

"And now," Elliot went on, "I am going to ask my brilliant partner to pick a card from this brand-new deck."

Elliot went on with the trick. First he blindfolded

himself. Then he spread out the cards and let Mary-Kate choose one. She held it up for Ashley and the audience to see.

After showing the card to the audience, Mary-Kate put it back in the deck.

Elliot went on, running through the whole trick. He held up various cards to Ashley.

"Sugar the Wonder Horse, is this Mary-Kate's card?" Elliot asked.

Ashley shook her head no.

Then he picked another card. "Is this it?"

Ashley shook her head no again.

"Good girl," Mary-Kate said, feeding Ashley a lump of sugar.

Everyone in the audience laughed harder.

"Hey!" Mary-Kate giggled as Ashley spit the sugar cube in her direction. But she could see that Ashley was laughing, too.

Finally, after some more hocus-pocus, Elliot opened a sealed envelope. "Is this your card?" he asked Ashley.

Ashley nodded her head yes.

Elliot turned to the audience of other magicians. "What did you think?" he asked.

"Your horse is kind of funny-looking," someone

called out from the seats. Everyone laughed.

"Yeah!" someone else said. "I hope it goes that well with the real horse."

Elliot looked hard at Mary-Kate. "So do I," he whispered.

"Don't worry," Mary-Kate replied. "I guarantee it will. Sugar won't let us down."

"What do you think?" Ashley asked Mary-Kate. "Too heavy on the sequins?"

Mary-Kate and Ashley were in Ashley's dorm room putting the finishing touches on their costumes.

Ashley twirled around to model the outfit she was wearing for the magic show that night—a pair of black tights and a long-sleeved black leotard. The arms and legs were decorated with colorful swirls of sequins.

Ashley had sewn a triple row of sequins around the ankles, since her feet were going to show more than anything else. Her hair was held back in a ponytail with a sequin-covered scrunchie.

"I like it," Mary-Kate said. "Besides, you always said there's no such thing as too many sequins."

"It's true," Ashley laughed. "Especially when it

comes to magicians' costumes. Wait until you see the fake feet!" she added. "They have sequins around the ankles, too. They look just like the real things."

She glanced down at the rabbit cage on the floor. The door was open—and the rabbit was gone.

Ashley sighed. "The rabbit escaped from his cage again! He's always doing that!"

Mary-Kate helped her search the room. "How does he open the door?" she asked.

"I have no idea," Ashley replied. "He's got to be in here somewhere." She opened the closet door.

Mary-Kate checked under the bed. "Here he is," she said, scooping the rabbit into her arms. "He was hiding behind the dust bunnies under your bed!"

"Ha-ha-ha." Ashley took the rabbit and put him back in the cage. "Now stay in there!" she ordered. She set a sneaker against the door to block it.

"Has Phoebe named him yet?" Mary-Kate asked.

Ashley shook her head. "She should name him Houdini," she said. "After that magician who was a famous escape artist."

"That's perfect!" Phoebe exclaimed as she slipped into the room. She hurried to the cage and wiggled her finger at the rabbit. "I've been trying to come up with a name for days. From now on we'll call him Houdini."

"Wow, Phoebe," Mary-Kate said. "You look awesome."

Phoebe was wearing a long satin skirt and the vintage fur-trimmed sweater. "I was trying to match the rabbit," Phoebe said, petting the white fur on her sweater.

"What are you going to do with Houdini once the show's over?" Mary-Kate asked. She knew Ashley didn't want the rabbit to stay in their room. He was cute, but they could get into trouble if Ms. Viola found him.

"Max's parents and little sister are coming to the show," Phoebe told her. "Max is going to let his sister keep Houdini." She sighed. "I'm going to miss him. But it's for the best."

"I have butterflies in my stomach," Mary-Kate confessed. "What if Sugar messes up Elliot's card trick?"

"What if I mess up in the magicians' box?" Ashley worried.

"None of us is going to mess up tonight," Phoebe said.

She looked at Mary-Kate's costume and smiled. Phoebe had lent her the vintage riding outfit: jodhpurs and black boots, and a lacy white silk blouse with ruffles on top.

"You look like a real horsewoman in that outfit," Phoebe said.

"Speaking of horses, how is Sugar getting to the show?" Ashley asked.

"Darcy called to say it's all set," Mary-Kate explained. "Sean is going to pick up Sugar at Darcy's stable and drive him to the show in his horse trailer."

"Sounds good!" Ashley said. She looked at her watch and gasped. "We'd better go. It's almost showtime."

There was a knock on the door. "Phoebe? Ashley?"

"It's Ms. Viola!" Phoebe whispered. She quickly shoved the rabbit cage behind the bed.

Phoebe nodded at Ashley, who called, "Come in."

Ms. Viola poked her head into the room. "Mary-Kate, there you are. You have a telephone call," she said. "It sounds important."

Who could it be? Mary-Kate wondered. "Thanks, Ms. Viola," she said.

"We'll meet you at the bus stop," Ashley said, putting on her jacket.

"Okay," Mary-Kate replied. She hurried out of the room to pick up the hall phone.

"Hello?" she said into the receiver.

"Mary-Kate?" a voice said. "It's Sean."

"Sean!" Mary-Kate said happily. "How's Sugar doing? Is he ready for his big debut?"

"That's why I'm calling," Sean said. "I have basketball practice at school tonight. So I asked J.D. to bring Sugar to the show. Is that okay?"

"Fine with me," Mary-Kate told Sean. "As long as someone brings him."

"Cool," Sean said. "Break a leg tonight. But not Sugar's."

Mary-Kate laughed. "Thanks." She hung up and hurried to catch up with Phoebe and Ashley at the shuttle bus.

When the girls reached the auditorium, the place was buzzing with excitement. Girls from White Oak were hanging out in the aisles, talking to the Harrington guys. There were lots of people Mary-Kate didn't recognize, many of them from the neighboring towns. Most of the Harrington and

White Oak faculty had turned out for the show, too. Mary-Kate saw her roommate, Campbell, and their friends Elise Van Hook and Samantha Kramer sitting in the third row. They smiled and gave the girls thumbs-up signs.

"We can't wait to see your acts!" Campbell cheered.

Phoebe and Ashley waved. "I have to go find my horse," Mary-Kate called. "I'll see you later!"

Backstage, students dressed in glittery costumes were running around collecting props. Mary-Kate saw magic wands, rings, ropes, and birds. She opened the back door to see if Sugar was waiting for her in the yard behind the auditorium. There was no sign of a horse anywhere.

"Hey, Mary-Kate," Elliot said, walking up to her and peering out the door. "Where's the star of the show?"

"He should be here any minute," Mary-Kate said nervously.

"Great." Elliot smiled and walked away.

Mary-Kate walked over to Ross and Ashley. Ross was wearing black jeans, a crisp white shirt, and a black cape.

"I've got something for you," Ross was saying to

Ashley. He reached into the pocket of his pants and pulled out a small white box tied with a red ribbon. "Open it," he said.

"A present?" Ashley asked. "What for?"

Ross glanced down at his feet. "I still felt bad about our fight," he said. "I just wanted to get you something to show how glad I am that we're partners."

"Wow, Ross," Ashley said. "That's so sweet." She untied the ribbon and lifted the lid. A pair of pretty silver earrings with pink stones rested on a little square of cotton in the box.

"Oh, Ross, I love them!" Ashley threw her arms around his neck and gave him a hug.

"For good luck," he said. "Our tricks are going to be great tonight. Both of them."

Ashley smiled as she put on the earrings. They looked beautiful on her. Mary-Kate was really happy for her sister.

Too bad she was a nervous wreck!

Mary-Kate went to peek outside again when she heard Jeremy starting his emcee speech.

Oh, no! Mary-Kate thought. The show was about to begin and Sugar was nowhere in sight!

CHAPTER NINE

Ashley hopped up and down with nervous excitement as she watched the show from the wings. Phoebe and Max got a big round of applause for their rabbit trick. And Marty Silver came up with a great mind-reading trick that totally dazzled the audience.

"Ashley!" Mary-Kate whispered. "Hide me!" She ducked down behind her sister.

"Mary-Kate, what are you doing?" Ashley asked.

"I can't let Elliot find me," Mary-Kate said. "J.D. hasn't brought Sugar yet. I tried calling the stables, but no one answered. What if they don't show up?"

Ashley shook her head sympathetically. "I'll

keep my fingers crossed. And I'll try to stall on my trick to give you more time."

From the stage, Jeremy was announcing the next act. "And now, Ross Lambert and his lovely partner, Ashley Burke!" he said.

"Ready?" Ross asked, coming up behind Ashley. Together, they pushed the box out onto the stage. Ashley beamed her brightest smile at the audience.

"Ladies and gentlemen," Ross said in a deep, serious voice. "I am going to need complete silence for the next few minutes, because the trick I am about to perform is extremely dangerous."

He kept talking while Ashley slipped into the box. When all the latches were locked, he twirled the table around. Now the audience couldn't see Ashley's feet, because they were facing the back of the stage.

Please let me switch the feet in time, Ashley silently prayed.

As fast as she could, she pulled her feet out of the holes and stuck the fake feet in. Then she pulled the lever and quickly lowered herself into the secret compartment.

I did it! Ashley thought. *That was my best time yet!*

Ross swung the table around and picked up the saw.

"This saw is so sharp," Ross said, "we have an

ambulance standing by outside, just in case!"

Ashley turned to the audience and faked a look of fright.

Ross placed the saw in the slit in the middle of the box. He sawed back and forth with huge sweeps.

"Ouch!" Ashley cried. She winked at Ross. The audience gasped.

"Not to worry," Ross said. "My partner won't feel a thing . . . after this!" He pulled the box apart in two pieces.

The crowd gasped even louder.

"Tada!" Ashley said. The audience cheered and clapped.

Then Ross swung the table around again. Ashley raised herself out of the secret compartment, switched the feet back, and hopped out of the box. The audience applauded again.

Ross smiled at Ashley. "You did a great job," he whispered.

"We make a great team," Ashley replied.

"Thank you," Ross said to the audience. "And now, Ashley is going to perform her famous tie-cutting trick and I'm going to assist her." Ross ran off the stage.

What's he doing? Ashley wondered. A second

later, she watched as he ran back onstage wearing a sequined T-shirt—that matched her costume!

The audience burst out laughing. Ashley gasped in surprise and then started laughing, too. He'd kept the matching T-shirt a secret—just to surprise her!

"How did you manage to match my costume?" she whispered to him.

"I've got spies," he replied, nodding at Phoebe, who watched from the wings.

Ross grinned and wheeled a small table up to the microphone. On the table was a big top hat. Inside the hat were the two secret pockets. In the left pocket was the duplicate of Mr. Barber's tie.

"For this trick I need a volunteer from the audience," Ashley said. She looked out into the crowd. "Mr. Barber, would you like to help me, please?"

Mr. Barber smiled and made his way to the stage.

"I have a question for the audience," Ashley went on. "Would anyone like to see Mr. Barber's tie cut in half?"

The crowd went totally wild. Everyone yelled and cheered. "Yeah!" they screamed.

Everyone except Mr. Barber. "You didn't tell me this would have anything to do with my tie." He frowned.

"Trust me," Ashley said, winking at him. "Would you take off your tie, please?"

Mr. Barber shook his head. "Sorry," he went on. "But this tie is really special to me. Nothing can happen to it."

"Bar-ber, Bar-ber, Bar-ber!" the audience chanted.

"Please, Mr. Barber," Ashley begged. "I promise nothing will happen to your tie."

Mr. Barber hesitated. "Okay," he said. "But I hope you know what you're doing."

The teacher gave Ashley his tie and she walked over to the table with the hat.

"As you can see," Ashley said, "this top hat is empty."

She turned the hat upside down to prove it. Then she placed Mr. Barber's tie in the hat and covered the hat with a big silk scarf.

"Now, thanks to my magical powers, I am able to create an energy field around the tie," Ashley said. "An energy field that will make it impossible to harm this tie, no matter what I do!"

She reached under the cloth and felt around inside the hat. Mr. Barber's tie was loosely draped inside. The duplicate tie was still tucked into the left pocket.

"Can you feel the energy?" Ashley asked the

73

audience. The audience cheered again.

She kept talking while she put the real tie in the right pocket. But just as she was about to pull the fake tie out of the left pocket—

"I'm sorry, Ashley," Mr. Barber said, grabbing the hat. "But I changed my mind. I can't let you do magic on my tie. It's too important to me."

"Mr. Barber," Ross said, putting an arm around his teacher. "Ashley is a trained professional. She'll get your tie back to you safe and sound."

Ross gently took the hat back from Mr. Barber. The teacher didn't say anything.

"Everything's fine, right, Ashley?" Ross said. He smiled at the audience.

"Right," Ashley said weakly. *The only problem,* she thought, *is that the hat's all turned around. How am I going to figure out which pocket is which?*

"All right," Ashley announced, whipping the scarf off. She pulled the tie from the left-hand pocket and lifted it out of the hat.

Quickly she took a huge pair of scissors and held them out to the audience. The audience cheered.

Ashley used the scissors to slowly cut the tie in half.

The audience screamed and cheered again, but Mr. Barber looked totally freaked out.

"Don't worry," Ashley told him. "The energy field will keep your tie safe."

She lifted the silk scarf and once again showed the audience that the hat was empty. Then she dropped the two pieces of the cut tie back into the hat. She covered it again with the scarf, and put her hands inside.

Quickly she pulled the whole tie out of the right pocket and stuffed the cut pieces of necktie into the left one.

"Harrington, repairington," she said.

With a flourish she yanked off the scarf and pulled out the uncut tie.

"Tada!" Ashley announced, waving Mr. Barber's necktie for the crowd to see.

The crowd cheered again. *I did it!* Ashley thought. *My trick was a big hit!*

But Mr. Barber didn't look impressed. In fact, he stared at the back of his tie, his face furious.

"You'd better have an explanation for this," he said. "Because that is *not* my tie!"

CHAPTER
TEN

The audience fell silent. "Wh-what do you mean?" Ashley stammered.

"This tie is a fake," Mr. Barber declared, taking the tie from Ashley. "The tie I wear to school every day was autographed on the back by Mick Jagger!" Mary-Kate watched her sister's magic act from the wings. Her stomach tensed up and did a flip-flop.

Oh, no, Mary-Kate thought. *This is horrible!*

"Mick Jagger's autograph?" Ashley asked. "As in Mick Jagger, the lead singer of the Rolling Stones?"

Mr. Barber nodded. "I sat next to him on an airplane once, thirty years ago. He signed the back of my tie. That's why I wear it all the time."

Oh, no! Mary-Kate thought. *Ashley's trick is ruined!*

"I'm so sorry," Ashley said. She reached into the hat and pulled out the two pieces of Mr. Barber's original tie. "I meant to cut the other one, but you grabbed the hat and . . . and the ties must have gotten mixed up."

Mr. Barber took the pieces back from Ashley. He turned them over and stared at the back.

Ashley's in big trouble now, Mary-Kate thought. *Mr. Barber is going to lose it!*

But to her surprise, Mr. Barber didn't lose it. Instead, he gave a little shrug and sighed.

"At least the autograph isn't cut," Mr. Barber said. "And I guess it's all for the best."

"The best?" Ashley asked, surprised.

"Yup," Mr. Barber said. "I guess thirty years is a long time. I was getting tired of wearing the same tie every day."

Ashley's eyes popped wide open.

"It's time to kiss the past good-bye!" Mr. Barber announced.

The audience went wild. Mary-Kate could see Ashley sigh with relief. But Mary-Kate's heart was still pounding in her chest. Her sister might be out of the woods, but *she* was in deep trouble. Sugar still wasn't there.

Elliot marched over to her. "Okay, where is he?" he demanded. "We can't go onstage without a horse!"

"I don't know," Mary-Kate said. "J.D. should have been here by now."

Ashley and Ross ran past them off the stage.

"All right!" Mary-Kate heard Jeremy announce onstage. "And now it's time for the grand finale. Let's hear it for Elliot Weber and Mary-Kate Burke!"

"Come on," Elliot said. He jerked his head. "We'll have to do the trick ourselves!"

But an instant later, the big back door opened. J.D. was standing there with Sugar in tow.

"Wow! Just in time!" Mary-Kate cried.

She grabbed the reins from J.D. and Elliot walked onto the stage. He took a bow.

"Thank you, thank you," Elliot said. "And now, ladies and gentlemen, we have an incredibly special treat for you. My partner and I are going to demonstrate that even a horse can do card tricks. Ready, Mary-Kate?"

That was Mary-Kate's cue to walk Sugar onto the

stage. She pulled on the horse's reins. But for some reason, the horse didn't move.

Mary-Kate got a sinking feeling in her stomach. She glanced down at the horse's ankle. Sure enough, there was the white patch.

Oh, no! Mary-Kate thought. *This is the wrong Sugar!*

CHAPTER ELEVEN

She hurried offstage and whispered to J.D., "Did you pick up this horse at Darcy's stables?"

J.D. looked confused. "No, why would I do that?" he asked.

Mary-Kate's heart pounded. She glanced back at the stage. Elliot was walking offstage toward them. "What's going on?" he asked.

"This is the wrong horse," Mary-Kate wailed. "There was a mix-up." She explained what happened to Elliot and J.D.

"We can't go onstage now!" Elliot exclaimed. "We'll make fools of ourselves."

Mr. Thornbush, one of the Harrington teachers,

walked by at that moment. "Don't be silly," he said. "You'll be great! You shouldn't have stage fright."

"But Mr. Thornbush, you don't understand—" Mary-Kate began.

"Now here we go. Onto the stage, the three of you." Mr. Thornbush took Sugar's reins and began to lead him onstage. Then he gave Mary-Kate and Elliot a little push in the same direction.

Mary-Kate glanced at Elliot. "It looks like we're doing this trick whether we want to or not," she whispered.

Elliot walked to the middle of the stage and slowly began his patter. "Sorry for the delay, folks," he announced. "But we're back, with Sugar . . . our wonder horse."

Mary-Kate wanted to melt into the floor.

"He's a really smart horse," Elliot went on. "I think you'll all be amazed to find out that Sugar can recognize all fifty-two cards in the deck!"

Elliot blindfolded himself so he couldn't see the cards. Then he spread out the deck of cards on the table, and told Mary-Kate to pick one.

Mary-Kate picked the six of diamonds and held it up for Sugar to see. Then she showed the card to the audience.

"What should I do now?" Mary-Kate asked Elliot.

"Put the card back in the deck anywhere you want," Elliot said.

Elliot went on with the act as he shuffled the cards. Then he finally pulled a three of clubs out of the deck.

He turned to face Sugar with the card in his right hand. "Is this your card?" Elliot asked the horse.

The horse just stood there.

Maybe I can help, Mary-Kate thought desperately. She nonchalantly strolled over to the horse and gave him a nudge.

The audience giggled.

"Maybe he's hard of hearing," Elliot joked. "Is this your card?" he said much louder.

Mary-Kate looked at Sugar and shook her head no. The audience laughed some more.

"Now, Sugar, I'm going to give you one more chance," Elliot said. He raised the card high and walked right up to Sugar's nose. "Is this the card Mary-Kate showed you?" he asked.

Sugar panicked. He started backing up, trying to get offstage. Mary-Kate grabbed his bridle but he kept moving.

The audience broke out in whispers. *This is hopeless,* Mary-Kate thought.

"Mary-Kate!" Ashley called from offstage. "Look!" She pointed to the door.

Mary-Kate glanced at the door. Then she gasped. Sean and Darcy were standing there. And with them was Darcy's horse!

Mary-Kate sighed with relief. *That's the Sugar I've been looking for.*

"Uh, ladies and gentlemen," Mary-Kate said, smiling. "As you can see, this horse isn't as smart as we thought he was. But in just a moment I plan to amaze you by transforming this dumb horse into a totally brilliant one!"

Everyone in the audience stopped whispering. Elliot opened his mouth to protest, but Mary-Kate quickly put her finger to her lips to shush him.

"All I need the audience to do is count to ten," she said.

The audience started counting. Mary-Kate signaled the stagehand to bring the curtain down.

"One! Two! Three! Four! Five!" she heard the audience say.

Mary-Kate waved to Sean to come and get the stubborn Sugar off the stage.

"What happened?" she asked him quickly.

"I realized I never told J.D. to go to Darcy's stables," Sean said quickly. "Big mistake. So here I am."

"Thank goodness!" Mary-Kate said.

She hurried to take the reins of Darcy's horse and bring the good Sugar onstage. Then she signaled to bring the curtain back up.

"Ladies and gentlemen, I think you will be amazed to experience the new brainpower of this horse," Mary-Kate said. "And now the great Elliot Weber will continue with his card trick."

"Um, right," Elliot said, pulling himself together. "Does everyone remember what the original card was?"

"Yes!" the audience shouted.

Elliot proceeded with the trick. First he held up his right hand and showed Sugar the three of clubs. "Is this your card?"

Sugar shook his head no, and the audience cheered.

Elliot showed him a ten of spades next. "Is this your card?" he asked Sugar.

Sugar shook his head no again. The audience clapped louder.

They love it! Mary-Kate thought happily.

"Is this your card?" Elliot asked, holding up a queen of hearts.

Sugar shook his head no. Mary-Kate could feel the audience sit up in their seats.

Elliot turned to the audience. "Ah!" he said. "I think I know what the problem is."

He walked over to the front of the stage and bent down. "Excuse me," he said to a woman sitting in the first row. "There's an envelope taped to the bottom of your chair. Could you hand it to me?"

The woman looked under her seat and gave him the envelope.

"Thank you," Elliot said.

He opened the envelope and took out a card. He showed it to Sugar. "Is this your card?" Elliot asked. He held it up with his left hand.

Sugar nodded his head up and down—and immediately Elliot spun around to show the card to the audience.

It was the six of diamonds. The right card!

The crowd went wild. Darcy jumped up and down in the wings, shouting, "That's my horse! That's my horse!"

"We did it!" Mary-Kate cheered, beaming with

pride. She was so excited she gave Sugar *and* Elliot a hug!

"Su-gar! Su-gar!" Mary-Kate heard the audience cheer.

A moment later, Jeremy leaped back onto the stage.

"Let's give it up for all our magicians tonight!" he said, motioning for everyone to come onstage and take a bow.

But the audience did more than applaud. They jumped to their feet and gave the whole show a standing ovation.

Wow! Mary-Kate thought. *We're a hit!*

Ashley ran over and put an arm around her sister. "You did it!" she cheered. "You were fabulous!"

"So were you!" Mary-Kate said.

Elliot nudged Mary-Kate. "Our trick was the best! I'll be your partner anytime, Mary-Kate."

"Thanks, Elliot," Mary-Kate said. "But it almost didn't work out. I can't believe I made it through that trick and survived!"

"Hey—I survived being cut in half!" Ashley joked. "And I survived my first fight with Ross."

Mary-Kate smiled at her sister. "Isn't it great when everything works out in the end?"

"Yeah," Ashley answered. "It's just like magic!"

ACORN

The Voice of White Oak Academy Since 1905

ABRACADABRA!
by Phoebe Cahill

What's the fastest way to make the winter blahs disappear? It's really easy—and you won't even need a magic wand to make it happen. Just show up at the Harrington magic show next Friday night!

The show is sure to be tons and tons of fun. Justin Martinez will amaze us with his coin tricks. Max Dorfman will make a bunny appear from a magic hat. And I'm not allowed to say what Elliot Weber is going to do—but I can tell you that it involves a mind-reading horse!

Rehearsals have been in full swing for a week now, with only two minor setbacks: Jessie Hamilton accidentally handcuffed himself to a chair in the auditorium—and forgot where he put the key!

But that stunt didn't top Seth Samuels' three-ring disaster. He was supposed to link and unlink three solid silver rings. But he wound up in the nurse's office because somehow, he got a ring stuck around his neck!

Anyway, most of the tricks are turning out to be a big hit. So make sure you don't miss the Harrington magic show! There are no tickets required—just say the magic word at the door. (Hint: It's the same magic word your mother taught you!)

GLAM GAB
by Ashley Burke and
Phoebe Cahill

shion expert Ashley Burke

Ready, girls? Reach into those closets, pull out those faded jeans, and toss them aside. Because this season

is screaming navy blue denim—and you don't want to be out of the loop on this one!

Can't save up the money to buy a new pair of jeans every time the styles change? Well this is one trend you won't have to miss out on. We've got a plan to keep your wardrobe up-to-date without breaking anyone's budget.

All you need is a pair of your old, faded jeans, a box of navy blue fabric dye, and a washing machine. Pop the jeans into the machine, pour in the dye, and follow the instructions on the box. You'll wind up with perfectly dark blue jeans—for a fraction of the price! But be sure to rinse out the washer when you're done. Otherwise, the next time you do laundry you'll wind up with dark blue everything!

THE GET-REAL GIRL

Dear Get-Real Girl,
My roommate thinks she's soooo cool because her boyfriend sent her fourteen valentines—one for every day of February until the big day. The cards are cluttering up the whole bul-

letin board in our room. Why should I have to look at all that mushy junk?

> Signed,
> Sick of Love

Dear Sick,
  Roses are red
  Violets are blue
  You're jealous of your roommate
  And lying about it, too!

Admit it: if you got fourteen valentines in fourteen days, you'd probably plaster them all over the walls, too!

Instead of complaining about your roommate, try sending out a few valentines of your own. Valentine's Day isn't about being grouchy—it's about spreading the love!

> Signed,
> Get-Real Girl

Dear Get-Real Girl,
Is it okay to gossip about someone who always gossips about me? I'm not naming any names, but this girl I know told everyone in my dorm that I'm hiding big bags of cookies and chips in my closet. Like it's any of her busi-

ness! How would she like it if I told everyone she snores like a chainsaw?

Signed,
Gonna Be a Big Mouth

Dear Big Mouth,
Forget the "Gonna Be." Your mouth is already big, and getting bigger! Tell the truth—this girl you're talking about isn't just

anybody—it's your roommate, right? Otherwise, she wouldn't know what you were hiding in your closet, and you wouldn't know she snores!

To solve this gossip problem, why don't you try talking *to* her rather than *about* her? Pull up a comfy chair, crack open one of those bags of chips you've been hiding, and have a heart-to-heart. Explain to

her that it bothers you when she spreads rumors about you—even if they *are* true!

If that doesn't work, just let me know and I'll print her name in this column. I get the feeling I know who you're talking about—my next-door neighbor snores so loud I can hear her right though the wall!

Signed,
Get-Real Girl

POLAR BEARS AT WHITE OAK!
by Mary-Kate Burke

Sports pro Mary-Kate Burke

You wouldn't believe it folks—but while you were trying to stay warm outside with scarves, hats, and mittens, yours truly was hanging out with a bunch of grown-ups who were wearing nothing but their bathing suits!

Who could have guessed that New Hampshire had its very own posse of Polar Bears? No I don't mean the furry white kind. I mean the kind who look like your grandparents and go swimming when it's freezing outside!

I got to check out the bears last Sunday when we all went down to Lake Lamar

for a swim. (Well, they all went for a swim, I watched from the sidelines while I sipped hot cocoa.) It was amazing to see the four men and three women in their bathing suits running right into the icy water. I got a chill just watching them!

But I did pick up a few new swimming strokes. The first is the "Time To Get Out Of This Lake" stroke. All you have to do is paddle your arms really really fast. (Some of the less enthusiastic Polar Bears did this one a lot.) There's also one I call the "Shiver Stroke." That's where you shake and swim at the same time. But I don't think that one has anything to do with the technique!

If you want to come and see the Polar Bears in action, they'll be down at the lake again next Sunday morning. And if you're feeling brave—bring your bathing suit!

THE FIRST FORM BUZZ

by Dana Woletsky

These days, it doesn't take a magic wand to stir up some gossip at White Oak. It's everywhere you look!

Things have been hopping in Porter House lately. Tell me, PC, do you know anything about a certain white

rabbit that wound up in EVH's fuzzy bathrobe last night? Apparently you should spend less time on your magic trick and more time on bunny patrol!

And come on, MKB—did you really think you could train a horse to do tricks? Please, you'll need more than a magic wand to pull

off that one in time for the show!

Speaking of the show, AB gave new meaning to the phrase "dumb as a horse," yesterday when she acted as a replacement horse in her sister's magic act. Although I have to say, she did manage to shake her head yes and no at all the right times. Maybe you're not as dumb as you look, AB!

That's it for the buzz. Remember my motto. If you want the scoop, you just gotta snoop!

UPCOMING CALENDAR
Winter / Spring

Get ready for the Roommate Blind Date Dance! That's right first-formers, it's time to set your roommates up on a blind date!

Is your roomie as sweet as sugar? Set her up with her secret crush. Don't get along with your roommate?

That nerdy guy in your math class probably needs a date to the dance! The sign-up sheet is hanging outside the Student U. Grab those pencils and get over there today!

Feeling lucky? There's going to be a St. Patty's Day party in the Student Union on March 15th.

Admission is $5.00. Wear something green and admission is half price. Bring a shamrock and you're in for free!

Has studying for midterms got you stressed? From 9:00-9:01 on Wednesday, it's officially Scream Your Head Off time! That's right, folks, throw those dorm windows open and let all those other students know—you feel their pain!

The April Fools' Day banquet this year has been canceled.

Just kidding! The annual Harrington/White Oak banquet will be held on April 1st as always. But

elections for King and Queen of the banquet are coming up soon. Entries to run must be in by March 24th.

IT'S ALL IN THE STARS
Winter Horoscopes

Aquarius
(January 21-February 19)

What will the future bring? That's a question for an Aquarius, because she has the ability to look beyond today—and come up with solutions for tomorrow.

Thanks to thinkers like you, your community is likely to be a better place. But don't forget to live in the moment every once in a while. After all—if you think too much about tomorrow, you might just miss today!

Pisces
(February 20-March 20)

Close your eyes, Pisces, and let yourself dream, since that's one of the things you like to do best. This month is special, because the stars are on your side and ready to make your dreams a reality. So the next time you have a dream—don't stop there. Work out a real plan to help it come true—and it will!

Aries
(March 21-April 19)

It may be cold outside, but you're ready to get all fired up this month, Aries. You want to leave your mark and find a way to change the world for the better. Great! Go for it! We know you can make it happen, cause you've got energy to burn!

Take a sneak peek
at

#22 April Fools' Rules!

"I can't believe I'm next!" Ashley Burke exclaimed, jumping up and down. In a few minutes, she would be onstage telling jokes in front of the whole seventh grade!

"You're going to be great," Mary-Kate said, putting an arm around her sister.

"Picture it, Mary-Kate," Ashley said dreamily. "Ross and I, together at the April Fools' Day Banquet as the king and queen!"

Ross Lambert was Ashley's boyfriend. Everyone thought he was a shoo-in to win the competition for King of Fools. And Ashley planned to be his queen!

Mary-Kate smiled. "But first you have to win this

competition," she pointed out. "Do you have your jokes ready?"

"Yup," Ashley said confidently. "I'm going to be funnier than all the other contestants put together!"

"And now for our next candidate," the announcer called, "let's welcome Porter House's own—Ashley Burke!"

"You're up!" Mary-Kate said. She gave her sister a hug. "Good luck."

Ashley walked onstage. She could hear her friends in the audience cheering her name. "Ashley! Ash-ley!"

This is going to be a piece of cake, she thought.

Ashley turned and grabbed the microphone. She looked out into the audience.

And then she froze. She couldn't remember any of her jokes!

What's happening to me? Ashley panicked, as her face turned beet red. *It's my one shot to be Queen of Fools—and I'm about to blow it!*

Here's an excerpt from our newest
Mary-Kate & Ashley series

so little time

#2 INSTANT BOYFRIEND

"We've got to have a party this week!" fourteen-year-old Chloe Carlson told her sister, Riley. "It's the only way to make sure our social lives get off to an amazing start this year!"

Riley dropped her backpack on the steps outside West Malibu High and turned to face Chloe. "Right," she agreed. "And we'll each have a special guy as our date."

"And who would those special guys be?" Their friend Sierra Pomeroy walked up the steps with her bass guitar. Sierra played in a cool band called The Wave.

"I know who I want to be my date," Chloe said dreamily.

"That's a given." Riley knew her sister was talking about Travis Morgan. With his short brown hair and bad-boy attitude, he was one of the hottest guys at West Malibu. "But I don't know who I'm going to ask," Riley continued. "I haven't met any cute boys lately."

"Even more reason to have the party!" Chloe added.

"What kind of guy are you looking for?" Sierra asked.

Riley thought for a minute. "I need someone nice. Someone fun to be with. Someone better than Daniel Pitowsky."

"Who's that?" Sierra asked.

"He's a guy I knew in junior high," Riley explained. "He goes to a private school now, but he called me up and asked me out last week. Ugh—it was the worst date of my life. He was so rude."

"What happened?" Sierra asked.

"We went to the movies, and he met up with a bunch of his buddies there," Riley explained. "He spent the whole time talking to them instead of me. And he bought himself popcorn, and didn't even offer me any!"

"Anyone would be better than Daniel Pitowsky," Chloe agreed.

"I need someone who's the opposite of him," Riley said. "Someone considerate, who actually wants to talk to me. And he has to be funny, too."

Sierra looked Riley in the eye. "I know a guy who's exactly what you're looking for," she said.

"Really?" Riley said.

"What's he like?" Chloe asked.

Sierra sighed. "He's so sweet. He'd walk you home, carry your books . . . and there's no doubt he'd make you laugh," she replied. "Actually, from what I heard, I think he has a crush on you."

"You're kidding!" Riley cried. "What's his name?"

"I'm not sure if I should tell you," Sierra replied. "Are you feeling open-minded today?"

"Definitely!" Riley said. "If he's that nice, I'd go out with him in a heartbeat! So tell me—who is it?"

Do you have all the Mary-Kate and Ashley books?

Turn the page to find out!

Reading Checklist

andashley

ingle one!

TWO of a kind™